Girls

Coloring Book

Color and Relax

Creative Designe Studio

Thank you for choosing our coloring book.

There are 50 unique pictures waiting for you to color, which have different levels of complexity.

We hope you will find some peace and serenity while coloring our coloring pictures.

Have fun!

This coloring book belongs to:

Name: _____

Let´s go!

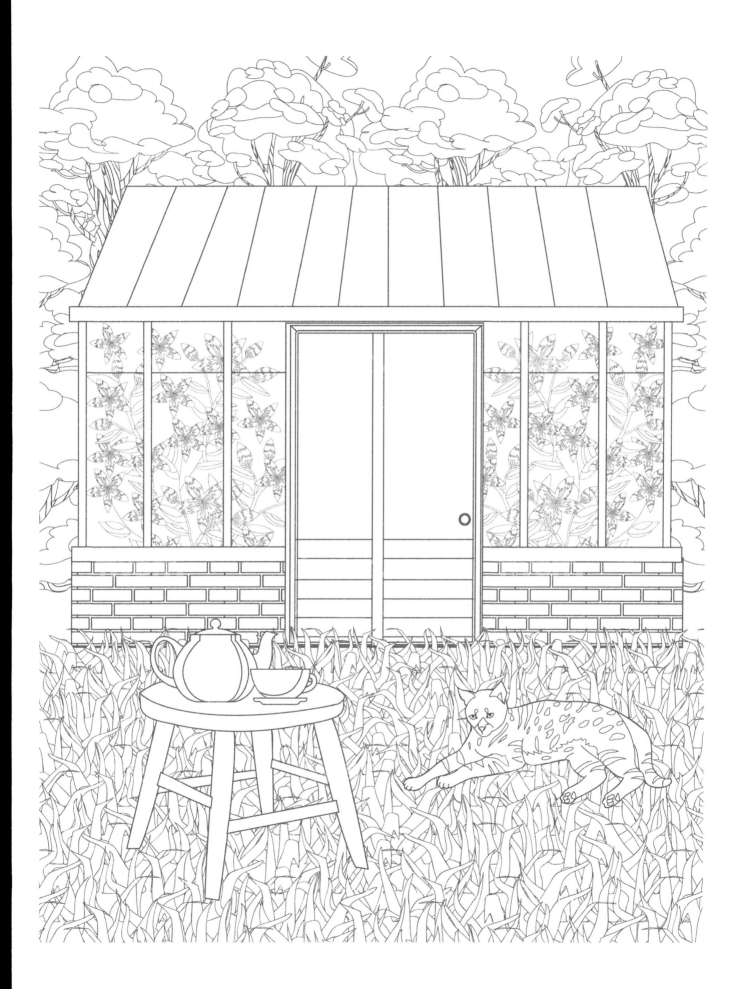

Σοφία

So, that's it unfortunately... ☺

We hope you had as much fun coloring as we had creating the pictures.

We would be delighted if you leave a positive review on Amazon

You can also look at our other products, maybe there is something for you.

Thank you for your trust in us and the purchase of this coloring book,

your Creative Designe Studio

Imprint

Made in the USA
Las Vegas, NV
21 December 2023

83386951R00063